MORGAN MORNING

Written By:
STEPHEN COSGROVE

Illustrated By
ROBIN JAMES

GROLIER ENTERPRISES INC.
Danbury, Connecticut

A Serendipity™ Book

Dedicated to the spirit and the being of a horse called Morgan.
May he live forever in the enchanted island of Robin's mind.

Stephen

Far beyond tomorrow lies an emerald island, where all things magical and real live together in perfect harmony . . . an island where the sun and moon come together to paint the sky the most amazing colors and hues . . . an island of bright and beautiful tomorrows.

At the very center of the island is a crystal glade called the Meadows of Morning. The glade is surrounded on all sides by tall and magnificent mountains. The only way in or out of the Meadows of Morning is along a narrow twisting trail that follows the river through the mountains.

It is here, protected from all harm, that creatures from all over the island come to give birth to their young. Mothers of every description, those with feathers or fur, long legs or wings, come to this quiet sanctuary to give birth to their babies.

It was in the early spring when the mountains were shedding their mantles of snow that a young colt was born in the deep grasses of the meadow. His mother had labored into the night, and just as the sun was peeking over the mountains, Morgan was born into the world.

He lay for a while, then stood on wobbily, shakey legs and gazed at all the wonders around him. He blinked his eyes in disbelief as the shadows fell away and all of nature looked at him.

Step by step, with his small tail swishing back and forth in nervous anticipation he explored bits and pieces of the meadow while his mother slept in the warm spring sunlight. With each step Morgan became a little more confident until he was walking without hardly falling at all.

Day by day his strength grew and so did his curiosity. Occasionally he would take off to chase a butterfly or a bee, and his mother would have to nicker for him to come back.

One day Morgan followed some squirrels across the meadow to their nest in the wide spreading oak. He was so intent on watching them gather nuts and berries that he didn't hear his mother's call. Finally, when his curiosity was satisfied, he walked back to where his mother was neighing impatiently.

"Morgan," she said as she nipped him on the ear, "some day your curiosity is going to get you in trouble. From now on you are to stay by my side at all times. Do you understand?"

Morgan dropped his head and muttered, "Yes, mom." For the rest of the day he stayed right at her side, but it wasn't much fun at all.

The next day the sunlight broke crisply on the Meadows of Morning. All the creatures, babies and mothers alike, rubbed the sleep from their eyes and went scurrying about the meadow searching for food. Morgan was no exception as he nibbled on the tender grasses that grew in the glade. For the longest time, he stayed at his mother's side as he had been told.

Suddenly, out of nowhere, five raccoons raced by with their tails sticking straight in the air. Without a thought or a glance back at his mother, Morgan raced after them. He didn't know where they were going, he just thought that it looked like a lot of fun.

He followed the bushy tails through the meadow and onto the path that ran beside the river between the feather ferns and golden green moss. On and on they raced, five little raccoons and Morgan, zipping down the twisted trail.

He had never had so much fun nor seen so many new things in all of his life! As they raced on, the river became swifter, and a roaring sound filled the air. Morgan rounded a twisted corner in the path, but the raccoons had disappeared as though they had vanished into thin air.

He looked up and down the trail, but there was no sign of his furry friends. Then, on the other side of the river, at the very edge of a cascading waterfall, Morgan saw the raccoons skipping from rock to rock across the raging river.

Without a thought for his safety, Morgan began walking on the stones set in the river. He was almost to the middle when he looked off to his side and saw the cascading waterfall. It went down and down a hundred feet or so and crashed with a large roar at the bottom.

He scrambled quickly to the next rock, but as fate would have it, his front hoof slipped on a bit of moss. Suddenly, Morgan found himself floating helplessly in the river as he was swept closer and closer to the brink of the waterfall.

"Mother!" he neighed with all his strength. But it was to no avail; he was carried over the edge!

Morgan fell for what seemed like an eternity. With water pouring all around him, he hit a boulder, bounced off and splashed into the cold, deep pool at the bottom. His leg hurt so, but with all the strength in his small body he pulled himself onto the sandy beach at the base of the falls.

He lay there for a time catching his breath and then tried to stand. As soon as he got to his feet, the leg that had hit the rock buckled and Morgan fell to the sand again. With tears streaming from his eyes, he suddenly realized that he was in more trouble than ever before.

With a few excited squeaks, the raccoons, who had been watching from high above, raced back to the meadow to find Morgan's mother.

His mother, along with all the other mothers and their babies, came and stood silently above the pool. There was no way for any of them to get down to help him, let alone guide him back up the waterfall.

Morgan's mother choked back a sob when she realized that nothing could be done. With tears streaming down her face, she walked silently away from the falls with all the other creatures following.

Morgan neighed softly and said, "I love you mother and I understand."

All alone now, the little colt lay in the cold sand with only the roar of the mighty waterfall to console him.

The damp, dark night settled about him as he slept fitfully, dreaming of other times and other places. Dreams of golden sunshine and brightly colored flowers. Dreams of running through meadows of clover. Dreams always ending the same: falling, falling through the mists of the falls and then to awaken and find that he was still all alone.

As the heavens began to brighten, the Morning Star lifted itself from the edge of the earth and began to rise majestically into the sky. The star rose and rose until, suddenly, it paused in mid-flight and a bright beacon of light shined down on the pathetic colt lying on the ground.

Morgan had just begun to blink his eyes in wonder when a booming voice called out to him, "Who are you, little horse, and why do you sleep on the cold, cold sand?"

"My name is Morgan," he said, "I am here because I didn't listen to my mother and foolishly fell from the rocks. Now I am waiting to die, for no one can help me." With that he began to cry and cry.

"Morgan," said the Morning Star, "we can help you. But . . . there are conditions."

"I'll do anything, anything at all!" cried Morgan.

"Listen first, little horse, and then decide. If we save you—and we will if you want—you will be banished from all others of your kind forever more. Never more will you be able to nuzzle next to your mother or her kind. For in order to save you, we must magically transform you into a unicorn. Thereafter, because you are of magic, you must live in a land of dreams and make-believe. As a sign of your pledge you will forever wear on your head a horn cast of purity and twilight wonder."

Morgan thought of a gentler time when he had played in the meadow and nuzzled his mother and others of his kind. But he knew that his only hope of living was to accept. With a lump in his throat and a deep sigh of regret, he agreed.

The bright beams of the Morning Star changed to all colors of the rainbow and the air sparkled with crystal delight. Morgan suddenly stood up. His leg was healed! In a burst of golden light the horn was affixed to his head for all of eternity . Then, as suddenly as it had appeared, the Morning Star faded from sight and Morgan, the unicorn, was left alone.

He slowly began to follow the river down to the meadowlands below, but he turned once more to look at the waterfall, and there stood his mother. "Good-bye, mother. I'll always love you," he neighed softly into the wind.

With a tearful eye, but a heart filled with hope for new adventure, Morgan turned and walked away.

INTO THIS LIFE
MORGAN WAS BORN
TO LIVE, MAYBE DIE,
AS A UNICORN